A Note to Parents and Teachers

Kids can imagine, kids can laugh and kids can learn to read with this exciting new series of first readers. Each book in the Kids Can Read series has been especially written, illustrated and designed for beginning readers. Humorous, easy-to-read stories, appealing characters, and engaging illustrations make for books that kids will want to read over and over again.

To make selecting a book easy for kids, parents and teachers, the Kids Can Read series offers three levels based on different reading abilities:

Level 1: Kids Can Start to Read

Short stories, simple sentences, easy vocabulary, lots of repetition and visual clues for kids just beginning to read.

Level 2: Kids Can Read with Help

Longer stories, varied sentences, increased vocabulary, some repetition and visual clues for kids who have some reading skills, but may need a little help.

Level 3: Kids Can Read Alone

Longer, more complex stories and sentences, more challenging vocabulary, language play, minimal repetition and visual clues for kids who are reading by themselves.

With the Kids Can Read series, kids can enter a new and exciting world of reading!

Franklin's Trading Cards

From an episode of the animated TV series *Franklin*,
produced by Nelvana Limited, Neurones France s.a.r.l. and
Neurones Luxembourg S.A., based on the Franklin books
by Paulette Bourgeois and Brenda Clark.

Story written by Sharon Jennings.

Illustrated by Sean Jeffrey, Alice Sinkner and Shelley Southern.

Based on the TV episode *Franklin and the Trading Cards*,
written by John Van Bruggen.

Kids Can Read is a trademark of Kids Can Press Ltd.

Franklin is a trademark of Kids Can Press Ltd.
The character Franklin was created by Paulette Bourgeois and Brenda Clark.
Text © 2003 Contextx Inc.
Illustrations © 2003 Brenda Clark Illustrator Inc.

Kids Can Press acknowledges the financial support of the Ontario Arts Council,
the Canada Council for the Arts and the Government of Canada, through the
BPIDP, for our publishing activity.

Published in Canada by   Published in the U.S. by
Kids Can Press Ltd.   Kids Can Press Ltd.
29 Birch Avenue   2250 Military Road
Toronto, ON M4V 1E2   Tonawanda, NY 14150

www.kidscanpress.com

Edited by Tara Walker
Designed by Stacie Bowes

Printed in Hong Kong, China, by Wing King Tong Company Limited

CM 03 0 9 8 7 6 5 4 3 2 1
CM PA 03 0 9 8 7 6 5 4 3 2 1

National Library of Canada Cataloguing in Publication Data

Jennings, Sharon
        Franklin's trading cards / Sharon Jennings ; illustrated by Sean Jeffrey, Alice
Sinkner, Shelley Southern.

(Kids Can read)
The character Franklin was created by Paulette Bourgeois and Brenda Clark.

ISBN 1-55337-463-0 (bound)   ISBN 1-55337-464-9 (pbk.)

I. Jeffrey, Sean II. Sinkner, Alice III. Southern, Shelley IV. Bourgeois, Paulette
V. Clark, Brenda VI. Title. VII. Series: Kids Can read (Toronto, Ont.)

PS8569.E563F783 2003   jC813'.54   C2002-904566-5
PZ7

Kids Can Press is a **ſ◎rʊs**™ Entertainment company

Franklin's Trading Cards

Kids Can Press

Franklin can tie his shoes.

Franklin can count by twos.

And Franklin can eat lots

and lots of cereal.

That's how he got all of the

Superhero Trading Cards.

Franklin ate breakfast every day.

Some days

he ate toast.

Some days

he ate pancakes.

But most days, he ate Fly Krispy cereal.

One day, Franklin found

two Superhero Trading Cards

in his cereal.

"Wow!" said Franklin.

"I will eat Fly Krispy every day."

Franklin told all of his friends

about Superhero Trading Cards.

Everyone began eating Fly Krispy cereal.

"I don't even like Fly Krispy," said Beaver.

"Me either," said Fox.

"But I want all the Superhero Trading Cards," said Beaver.

"Me too," said Fox.

Soon, Franklin had lots of Superhero
Trading Cards.

"I have Super Dog and Super Cow,"
said Franklin.

"Me too," said Beaver.

"I have Super Pig and Super Chicken,"
said Franklin.

"Me too," said Fox.

"But I do not have Super Cat,"

said Franklin.

Neither did Beaver or Fox.

One morning, Franklin had a good idea.

"I've found the trading cards

in this box of cereal," he told his mother.

"Please buy another box."

"Finish this box first," said his mother.

"Then I will buy more."

"Hmm," said Franklin.

"Then I will have two bowls of cereal

for breakfast."

At lunchtime, Franklin had a better idea.

"I will eat Fly Krispy cereal

for lunch and supper," he said.

Then Franklin had his best idea yet.

"I will make Fly Krispy squares

for dessert," he said.

"You will get tired of Fly Krispy cereal,"

said his mother.

"Never," said Franklin. "I love Fly Krispy."

After supper, Franklin went to see

his friends.

"I have eaten five boxes

of Fly Krispy cereal

in one week," he told them.

"And I still don't have Super Cat."

"Neither do I," said Beaver.

"But I have three Super Dogs."

"I have two Super Chickens," said Fox.

"But I don't have one Super Cat."

"Super Cat is hard to get," said Franklin.

The next day, Franklin opened

a new box of Fly Krispy.

He dug into the box.

"Hooray!" said Franklin.

"I got Super Cat!"

SUPER CAT

He dug in again.

"Wow!" said Franklin.

"Another Super Cat!"

Franklin ran to tell his friends.

"Can I have the other Super Cat?"

asked Beaver and Fox together.

"I asked first," said Beaver.

"No, *I* asked first," said Fox.

Franklin didn't know what to do.

The next day at school,

Fox had an idea.

"I will trade my candy bar

for your Super Cat,"

he told Franklin.

Beaver had a better idea.

"I will trade two candy bars

for your Super Cat,"

she told Franklin.

Franklin still didn't know what to do.

After school, Franklin went to

the ice cream shop.

Fox and Beaver followed him.

"I will trade you an ice cream cone

for Super Cat," said Fox.

"I will trade you an ice cream cone

with two scoops

for Super Cat," said Beaver.

"Three scoops," said Fox.

"Four," said Beaver.

"I don't want that much ice cream,"

said Franklin.

Fox and Beaver did not listen.

Franklin went home to think.

"I don't know what to do,"

he told his mother.

"Beaver and Fox are both my friends."

"Why don't you flip a coin?" she said.

"Good idea!"
said Franklin.
"That's what
I will do."

"And I will stop buying Fly Krispy cereal,"
said his mother.
"You have a full set of Superhero
Trading Cards."

"That is *not*
a good idea,"
said Franklin.

The next day, Franklin went

to find Beaver.

He gave her one Super Cat Trading Card.

Beaver jumped up and down.

"Yippee!" she said.

"Now I don't have to eat Fly Krispy cereal

ever again."

Then Franklin went to find Fox.

He gave him the other Super Cat

Trading Card.

Fox jumped up and down.

"Yippee!" he said.

"Now I don't have to eat Fly Krispy cereal

ever again."

Franklin went home.

He opened a new box of

Fly Krispy cereal.

He dug into the box and found his

two trading cards.

Neither one was Super Cat.

"Yippee!" said Franklin.

"Maybe I will have to eat

Fly Krispy cereal forever."